**"In the soft earth was the imprint
of human feet!"**

THE LAST AMERICAN

Publisher's Note

America destroyed by cataclysmic climate change.

If you were to read a book written today that claims that the future of America might just be that, I am sure that you would not be surprised at all considering how much global warming and climate change are at the forefront of issues confronting us. However, this work is not new, and in fact was written over one hundred years ago by John Ames Mitchell (1845-1918), the founder and publisher of *Life* magazine.

Mitchell was a man of many talents. Educated at Phillips Exeter Academy, he later studied at the Lawrence Scientific School at Harvard. After leaving Harvard, Mitchell went on to study architecture in Boston and then at the *École des Beaux Arts* in Paris. He later returned to the U.S. where he would then work for an architecture firm for a number of years. John Ames returned to Paris again after deciding architecture was not his calling and there studied drawings and paintings at Julian's atelier and with Albert Maignan. Returning in 1880 to New York City, Mitchell founded *Life* magazine in 1883, which was a humorous weekly that was closer in its format to the New Yorker Magazine of today than the picture magazine that Henry Luce developed *Life* into when he bought the magazine in 1936. In addition to being an architect, artist, editor and novelist, Mitchell was also active in charitable work. In fact, he along with Horace Greely created the Fresh Air Fund.

J.A. Mitchell wrote fourteen books, the most famous being *Amos Judd*, which was made into the 1922 silent film, *The Young Rajah*, starring Rudolph Valentino.

The Last American was originally written in 1889, though this edition reprints the text and illustrations from the 1902 edition. The work is a quick though somewhat unsettling read, which begins in Persia with the reader joining a group of travelers who voyage across the ocean to find the remains of a once great nation called "Merhika."

Landing first in "Nhū-Yok" and later then in Washington, the reader follows these travelers as they make their way about the ruins, all the while commenting and comparing Persian society with the lost American society that they have found — a society, a race of people that they saw as "purely imitative; simply an enlarged copy of other nationalities extant at the time." A society that was obsessed with pleasure and money, with their chief passion being "to buy and sell."

And also a society that suddenly disappeared as a result of *"frightful climatic changes which swept the country like a mower's scythe."*

Though the story was no doubt written as a commentary on American society at the time, its tale can still be somewhat bothersome to the reader of today, especially and as noted above, when one considers how much global warming and climate change are at the forefront of issues facing America and other countries around the world. And also in light of our current relations with Iran.

— *Patrick Murdock*

The Last American

Published by Murdock Publishing Company

Copyright © 2006 by Murdock Publishing Company

Cover and interior layout and design
Kathy Harestad
www.kathyart.com

The text is an unabridged reprint from the 1902 edition of J.A. Mitchell's
The Last American, published by Frederick A. Stokes Company.
All the original illustrations from 1902 are included, however, the
color illustrations of F.W. Read appear in this edition as black and white.

For additional information about Murdock Publishing Company,
please write to:

Murdock Publishing Company
127 Belk Court • Clayton, NC 27520 USA
info@murdockmedia.com
www.murdockmedia.com

ISBN: 1-934102-04-0
ISBN-13: 978-1-934102-04-6

Printed in Quebec, Canada
by
Transcontinental Métrolitho

The Last American

A Fragment
FROM THE JOURNAL OF KHAN-LI,
*Prince of Dimph-Yoo-Chur
and Admiral in the Persian Navy*

ORIGINAL PAINTINGS BY F.W. READ
WITH DECORATIVE DESIGNS BY ALBERT D. BLASHFIELD
AND ILLUSTRATIVE DRAWINGS BY THE AUTHOR

MURDOCK PUBLISHING COMPANY

DRAWINGS

PAINTINGS

To
THOSE THOUGHTFUL PERSIANS
who can read a warning in the sudden rise
and swift extinction of a foolish people
this volume is dedicated.

A FEW WORDS
BY
HEDFUL

A FEW WORDS BY

HEDFUL

SURNAMED "THE AXIS OF WISDOM"

*Curator, of the Imperial Museum at Shiraz. Author of
"The Celestial Conquest of Kaly-phorn-ya," and of
"Northern Mehrika under the Hy-Bernyan Rulers"*

THE astounding discoveries of Khan-li of Dimph-yoo-chur have thrown floods of light upon the domestic life of the Mehrikan people. He little realized when he landed upon that sleeping continent what a service he was about to render history, or what enthusiasm his discoveries would arouse among Persian archaeologists.

Every student of antiquity is familiar with these facts.

But for the benefit of those who have yet to acquire a knowledge of this extraordinary people, I advise, first, a visit to the Museum at Teheran in order to excite their interest in the subject, and second, the reading of such hooks as Nōfūhl's "What we Found in the West," and Nōz-yt-ahl's "History of the Mehrikans." The last-named is a complete and reliable history of these people from the birth of the Republic under George-wash-yn-tun to the year 1990, when they ceased to exist as a nation. I must say, however, that Nōz-yt-ahl leaves the reader much confused concerning the period between the massacre of the Protestants in 1927, and the overflow of the Murfey dynasty in 1940.

He holds the opinion with many other historians that the Mehrikans were a mongrel race, with little or no patriotism, and were purely imitative; simply an enlarged copy of other nationalities extant at the time. He pronounces them a shallow, nervous, extravagant people, and accords them but few redeeming virtues. This, of course, is just; but nevertheless they will always be an interesting study by reason of their rapid growth, their vast numbers, their marvellous mechanical ingenuity and their sudden and almost unaccountable disappearance.

The wealth, luxury, and gradual decline of the native population; the frightful climatic changes which swept the country like a mower's scythe; the rapid conversion of a vast continent, alive with millions of pleasure-loving people, into a silent wilderness, where the sun and moon look down in turn upon hundreds of weed-grown cities, — all this is told by Nōz-yt-ahl with force and accuracy.

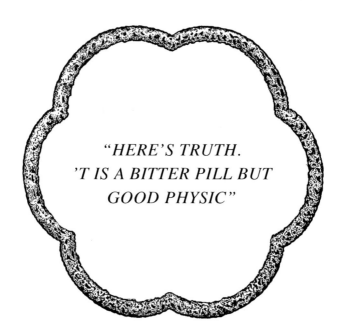

*"HERE'S TRUTH.
'T IS A BITTER PILL BUT
GOOD PHYSIC"*

ABOARD THE ZLŌTUHB
IN THE YEAR 2951

10th May

HERE is land ahead!

Grip-til-lah was first to see it, and when he shouted the tidings my heart beat fast with joy. The famished crew have forgotten their disconsolate stomachs and are dancing about the deck. 'T is not I, forsooth, who shall restrain them! A month of emptiness upon a heavy sea is preparation for any folly. Nōfūhl alone is without enthusiasm. The old man's heart seems dead.

THE LAST AMERICAN

We can see the land plainly, a dim strip along the western horizon. A fair wind blows from the northeast, but we get on with cruel hindrance, for the *Zlōtuhb* is a heavy ship, her bluff bow and voluminous bottom ill fitting her for speed.

The land, as we near it, seems covered with trees, and the white breakers along the yellow beach are a welcome sight.

11th May

IGHTED a fine harbor this afternoon, and are now at anchor in it.

Grip-til-lah thinks we have reached one of the western islands mentioned by Ben-a-Bout. Nōfūhl, however, is sure we are further North.

12th May

HAT a change has come over Nōfūhl! He is the youngest man aboard. We all share his delight, as our discoveries are truly marvellous. This morning while I was yet in my bunk he ran into the cabin and, forgetting our difference in rank, seized me by the arm and tried to drag me out. His excitement so had the better of him that I captured little meaning from his words. Hastening after him, however, I was amazed to see such ancient limbs transport a man so rapidly. He skipped up the narrow stairs like a heifer and, young though I am, it was faster than I could follow.

But what a sight when I reached the deck! We saw nothing of it yesterday, for the dusk of evening was already closing about us when we anchored.

Right ahead, in the middle of the bay, towered a gigantic statue, many times higher than the masts of our ship. Beyond, from behind this statue, came the broad river upon whose waters we were floating, its surface all a-glitter with the rising sun. To the East, where Nōfūhl was pointing, his fingers trembling with excitement, lay the ruins of an endless city. It stretched far away into the land beyond, further even than our eyes could see. And in the smaller river on the right stood two colossal structures, rising high in the air, and standing like twin brothers, as if to guard the deserted streets beneath. Not a sound reached us — not a floating thing disturbed the surface of the water. Verily, it seemed the sleep of Death.

I was lost in wonder.

As we looked, a strange bird, like a heron, arose with a hoarse cry from the foot of the great image and flew toward the city.

"What does it all mean?" I cried. "Where are we?"

THE LAST AMERICAN

"We soon found ourselves in what
was once a public square."

13

"Where indeed!" said Nōfūhl. "If I knew but that, O Prince, I could tell the rest! No traveller has mentioned these ruins. Persian history contains no record of such a people. Allah has decreed that we discover a forgotten world."

Within an hour we landed, and found ourselves in an ancient street, the pavements covered with weeds, grass, and flowers, all crowding together in wild neglect. Huge trees of great antiquity thrust their limbs through windows and roofs and produced a mournful sight. They gave a welcome shade, however, as we find the heat ashore of a roasting quality most hard to bear. The curious buildings on either side are wonderfully preserved, even sheets of glass still standing in many of the iron window-frames.

We wandered along through the thick grass, Nōfūhl and I, much excited over our discoveries and delighted with the strange scene. The sunshine is of dazzling brightness, birds are singing everywhere, and the ruins are gay

THE CITY OF RUINS

with gorgeous wild flowers. We soon found ourselves in what was once a public square, now for the most part a shady grove.[1]

As we sat on a fallen cornice and gazed on the lofty buildings about us I asked Nōfūhl if he was still in ignorance as to where we were, and he said:

"As yet I know not. The architecture is much like that of ancient Europe, but it tells us nothing."

Then I said to him in jest, "Let this teach us, O Nōfūhl! the folly of excessive wisdom. Who among thy pupils of the Imperial College at Ispahan would believe their venerable instructor in history and languages could visit the largest city in the world and know so little about it!"

"Thy words are wise, my Prince," he answered; "few babes could know less."

As we were leaving this grove my eyes fell upon an upturned slab that seemed to have

[1] Afterward ascertained to be the square of the City Hall.

a meaning. It was lying at our feet, partly hidden by the tall grass, having fallen from the columns that supported it. Upon its surface were strange characters in bold relief, as sharp and clear as when chiselled ten centuries ago. I pointed it out to Nōfūhl, and we bent over it with eager eyes. It was this:

ASTOR HOUSE

"The inscription is Old English," he said. " 'House' signified a dwelling, but the word 'Astor' I know not. It was probably the name of a deity, and here was his temple."

This was encouraging, and we looked about eagerly for other signs.

Our steps soon brought us into another street, and as we walked I expressed my surprise at the wonderful preservation of the stone work, which looked as though cut but yesterday.

"In such an atmosphere decay is slow," said Nōfūhl. "A thousand years at least have passed since these houses were occupied.

Take yonder oak, for instance; the tree itself has been growing for at least a hundred years, and we know from the fallen mass beneath it that centuries had gone by before its birth was possible."

He stopped speaking, his eyes fixed upon an inscription over a doorway, partly hidden by one of the branches of the oak. Turning suddenly upon me with a look of triumph, he exclaimed:

"It is ours!"

"What is ours?" I asked.

"The knowledge we sought;" and he pointed to the inscription,

NEW YORK STOCK EXC....

He was tremulous with joy.

"Thou hast heard of Nhū-Yok, O my Prince ?"

I answered that I had read of it at school.

"Thou art in it now!" he said. "We are standing on the Western Continent. Little

" 'The knowledge we sought;' and he
pointed to the inscription."

wonder we thought our voyage long!"

"And what was Nhū-Yok?" I asked. "I read of it at college, but remember little. Was it not the capital of the ancient Mehrikans?"

"Not the capital," he answered, "but their largest city. Its population was four millions."

"Four millions!" I exclaimed. "Verily, O Fountain of Wisdom, that is many for one city!"

"Such is history, my Prince! Moreover, as thou knowest, it would take us many days to walk this town."

"True, it is endless."

He continued thus: "Strange that a single word can tell so much! Those iron structures, the huge statue in the harbor, the temples with pointed towers, all are as writ in history."

Whereupon I repeated that I knew little of the Mehrikans save what I had learned at college, a perfunctory and fleeting knowledge,

IN A STREET OF THE FORGOTTEN CITY

as they were a people who interested me but little.

"Let us seat ourselves in the shade," said Nōfūhl, "and I will tell thee of them."

We sat.

"For eleven centuries the cities of this sleeping hemisphere have decayed in solitude. Their very existence has been forgotten. The people who built them have long since passed away, and their civilization is but a shadowy tradition. Historians are astounded that a nation of an hundred million beings should vanish from the earth like a mist, and leave so little behind. But to those familiar with their lives and character surprise is impossible. There was nothing to leave. The Mehrikans possessed neither literature, art, nor music of their own. Everything was borrowed. The very clothes they wore were copied with ludicrous precision from the models of other nations. They were a sharp, restless, quick-witted, greedy race, given body and soul to the gathering of riches. Their chiefest passion was to buy and sell. Even women, both of high and low degree, spent much of their time at bargains, crowding and jostling each other in vast marts of trade, for their attire was complicated, and demanded most of their time."

"How degrading!" I exclaimed.

"So it must have been," said Nōfūhl; "but they were not without virtues. Their domestic life was happy. A man had but one wife, and treated her as his equal."

"That is curious! But as I remember, they were a people of elastic honor."

"They were so considered," said Nōfūhl; "their commercial honor was a jest. They were sharper than the Turks. Prosperity was their god, with cunning and invention for his prophets. Their restless activity no Persian can comprehend. This vast country was alive with noisy industries, the nervous Mehrikans darting with inconceivable rapidity from one city to another by a system of locomotion we can only guess at. There existed roads with iron rods upon them, over which small houses on wheels were drawn with such velocity that a long day's journey was accomplished in an hour. Enormous ships without sails, driven by a mysterious force, bore hundreds of people at a time to the furthermost points of the earth."

"And are these things lost?" I asked. "We know many of the forces," said Nōfūhl, "but the knowledge of applying them is gone. The very elements seem to have been their slaves. Cities were illuminated at night by artificial moons, whose radiance eclipsed the moon above. Strange devices were in use by which they conversed together when separated by a journey of many days. Some of these appliances exist to-day in Persian museums. The superstitions of our ancestors allowed their secrets to be lost during those dark centuries from which at last we are waking."

At this point we heard the voice of Bhoz-jā-khāz in the distance; they had found a spring and he was calling to us.

Such heat we had never felt, and it grew hotter each hour. Near the river where we ate it was more comfortable, but even there the perspiration stood upon us in great drops. Our faces shone like fishes. It was our wish to explore further, but the streets were like ovens, and we returned to the *Zlōtuhb*.

As I sat upon the deck this afternoon recording the events of the morning in this journal Bhoz-jā-khāz and Ad-el-pate approached, asking permission to take the small boat and visit the great statue. Thereupon Nōfūhl informed us that this statue in ancient times held aloft a torch illuminating the whole harbor, and he requested Ad-el-pate to try and discover how the light was accomplished.

They returned toward evening with this information: that the statue is not of solid bronze, but hollow; that they ascended by means of an iron stairway into the head of the image, and from the top looked down upon us; that Ad-el-pate, in the dark, sat to rest himself upon a nest of yellow flies with black stripes; that these flies inserted stings into Ad-el-pate's person, causing him to exclaim loudly and descend the stairs with unexpected agility; that Bhoz-jā-khāz and the others pushed on through the upraised arm, and stood at last upon the bronze torch itself; that the city lay beneath them like a map, covering the country for miles away on both sides of the river. As for illuminating the harbor, Bhoz-jā-khāz says Nōfūhl is mistaken; there are no vestiges of anything that could give a light — no vessel for oil or traces of fire.

Nōfūhl says Jā-khāz is an idiot; that he shall go himself.

"The great statue in the harbor."

STARTLING discovery this morning.

By landing higher up the river we explored a part of the city where the buildings are of a different character from those we saw yesterday. Nōfūhl considers them the dwellings of the rich. In shape they are like bricks set on end, all very similar, uninteresting, and monotonous.

We noticed one where the doors and shutters were still in place, but rotting from the fantastic hinges that supported them. A few hard blows brought down the outer doors in a dusty heap, and as we stepped upon the marble floor within our eyes met an unexpected sight. Furniture, statues, dingy pictures in crumbling frames, images in bronze and silver, mirrors, curtains, all were there, but in every condition of decay. We knocked open the iron shutters and let the light into the rooms sealed up for centuries. In the first one lay a rug from Persia! Faded, moth-eaten, gone in places, it seemed to ask us with dying eyes to be taken hence. My heart grew soft over the ancient rug, and I caught a foolish look in Lev-el-Hedyd's eye.

As we climbed the mouldering stair to the floor above I expressed surprise that cloth and woodwork should hold together for so many centuries, also saying:

"These Mehrikans were not so unworthy as we think them."

"That may be," said Lev-el-Hedyd, "but the Persian rug is far the freshest object we have seen, and that perchance was ancient when they bought it."

On this floor we entered a dim chamber, spacious and once richly furnished. When Lev-el-Hedyd pushed open the shutters and drew aside the ragged curtains we started at the sight before us. Upon a wide bed in the centre of the room lay a human form, the long, yellow hair still clinging to the head. It was more a mummy than a skeleton. Around, upon the bed, lay mouldering fragments of the once white sheets that covered it. On the fingers of the left hand glistened two rings which drew our attention. One held a diamond of great price, the other was composed of sapphires and diamonds most curiously arranged. We stood a moment in silence, gazing sadly upon the figure.

"Poor woman," I said, "left thus to die alone."

"It is more probable," said Nōfūhl, "she was already dead, and her friends, departing perhaps in haste, were unable to burn the body."

"Did they burn their dead?" I asked. "In my history 't was writ they buried them in the earth like potatoes, and left them to rot."

And Nōfūhl answered: "At one time it was so, but later on, as they became more civilized, the custom was abandoned."

31

"Is it possible?" I asked, "that this woman has been lying here almost a thousand years and yet so well preserved?"

"I, also, am surprised," said Nōfūhl. "I can only account for it by the extreme dryness of the air in absorbing the juices of the body and retarding decay."

Then lifting tenderly in his hand some of the yellow hair, he said:

"She was probably very young, scarce twenty."

"Were their women fair?" I asked.

"They were beautiful," he answered; "with graceful forms and lovely faces; a pleasure to the eye; also were they gay and sprightly with much animation."

Thereupon cried Lev-el-Hedyd:

"Here are the first words thou hast uttered, O Nōfūhl, that cause me to regret the extinction of this people! There is ever a place in my heart for a blushing maiden!"

"Then let thy grief be of short life," re-

In the Mouldering Chamber

sponded Nōfūhl, "for Mehrikan damsels were
not of that description. Blushing was an art
they practised little. The shyness thou so
lovest in a Persian maiden was to them an unknown thing. Our shrinking daughters bear no
resemblance to these Western products. They
strode the public streets with roving eyes and
unblushing faces, holding free converse with
men as with women, bold of speech and free of
manner, going and coming as it pleased them
best. They knew much of the world, managed
their own affairs, and devised their own mar-
riages, often changing their minds and marry-
ing another than the betrothed."

"Bismillah! And men could love these
things?" exclaimed Lev-el-Hedyd with much
feeling.

"So it appears."

"But I should say the Mehrikan bride had
much the freshness of a dried fig."

"So she had," said Nōfūhl; "but those
who know only the dried fig have no regret for
the fresh fruit. But the fault was not with the

34

maidens. Brought up like boys, with the same studies and mental development, the womanly part of their nature gradually vanished as their minds expanded. Vigor of intellect was the object of a woman's education."

Then Lev-el-Hedyd exclaimed with great disgust: "Praises be to Allah for his aid in exterminating such a people!" and he walked away from the bed, and began looking about the chamber. In a moment he hastened back to us, saying:

"Here are more jewels! also money!"

Nōfūhl eagerly took the pieces.

"Money!" he cried. "Money will tell us more than pages of history!"

There were silver coins of different sizes and two small pieces of copper. Nōfūhl studied them closely.

"The latest date is 1957," he said; "a little less than a thousand years ago; but the piece may have been in circulation some years before this woman died; also it may have been

THE FACE AND BACK OF ONE OF THE SILVER COINS

coined the very year of her death. It bears the head of Dennis, the last of the Hy-Burnyan dictators. The race is supposed to have become extinct before 1990 of their era."

I then said: "Thou hast never told us, O Nōfūhl! the cause of their disappearance."

"There were many causes," he answered. "The Mehrikans themselves were of English origin, but people from all parts of Europe came here in vast numbers. Although the original comers were vigorous and hardy the effect of climate upon succeeding generations was fatal. They became flat-chested and thin, with scanty hair, fragile teeth, and weak digestions. Nervous diseases unknown to us wrought deadly havoc. Children we're reared with difficulty. Between 1945 and 1960, the last census of which any record remains, the population decreased from ninety millions to less than twelve millions. Climatic changes, the like of which no other land ever experienced, began at that period, and finished in less than ten years a work made easy by nervous natures and rapid lives. The temperature would skip in a single day from burning heat to winter's cold. No constitution could withstand it, and this vast continent became once more an empty wilderness."

Much more of the same nature he told us, but I am too sleepy to write longer. We explored the rest of the mansion, finding many things of interest. I caused several objects to be carried aboard the *Zlōtuhb*.[1]

[1] These objects are now in the museum of the Imperial College, at Teheran.

THE LAST AMERICAN

38

14th May

OTTER than yesterday.

In the afternoon we were rowed up the river and landed for a short walk. It is unsafe to brave the sun.

The more I learn of these Mehrikans the less interesting they become. Nōfūhl is of much the same mind, judging from our conversation today, as we walked along together.

It was in this wise:

Khan-li.

How alike the houses! How monotonous!

Nōfūhl.

So, also, were the occupants. They thought alike, worked alike, ate, dressed and

39

conversed alike. They read the same books; they fashioned their garments as directed, with no regard for the size or figure of the individual, and copied to a stitch the fashions of Europeans.

Khan-li.

But the close-fitting apparel of the European must have been sadly uncomfortable in the heat of a Mehrikan summer.

Nōfūhl.

So probably it was. Stiff boxes of varying patterns adorned the heads of men. Curious jackets with tight sleeves compressed the body. The feet throbbed and burned in close-fitting casings of unyielding leather, and linen made stiff by artificial means was drawn tightly about the neck.

Khan-li.

Allah! What idiots!

Nōfūhl.

Even so are they considered.

Khan-li.

To what quality of their minds do you attribute such love of needless suffering?

Nōfŭhl.

It was their desire to be like others. A natural feeling in a vulgar people.

15th May

 FAIR wind from the West to-day. We weighed anchor and sailed up the Eastern side of the city. I did this as Nōfūhl finds the upper portion of the town much richer in rel-ics than the lower, which seems to have been given up to commercial purposes. We sailed close under one of the great monuments in the river, and are at a loss to divine its meaning. Many iron rods still dangle from the tops of each of the structures. As they are in a line, one with the other, we thought at first they might have been once connected and served as a bridge, but we soon saw they were too far apart.

Came to anchor about three miles from the

old mooring. Up the river and down, North, South, East, and West, the ruins stretch away indefinitely, seemingly without end.

Am anxious about Lev-el-Hedyd. He went ashore and has not returned. It is now after midnight.

THE TWO MONUMENTS ON THE RIVER

16th May

PRAISE Allah! my dear comrade is alive! This morning we landed early and began our search for him. As we passed before the building which bears the inscription

. . . DORF ASTORIA

upon its front, we heard his voice from within in answer to our calls. We entered, and after climbing the ruined stairway found him seated upon the floor above. He had a swollen leg from an ugly sprain, and various bruises were also his. While our friends were constructing a litter on which to bear him hence we conversed together. The walls about us bore traces of having once enclosed a hall of some beauty. In idling about I pulled open

47

the decaying door of an old closet and saw upon the rotting shelves many pieces of glass and earthenware of fine workmanship. Taking one in my hand, a small wine-cup of glass, I

approached my comrade calling his attention to its slender stem and curious form. As his eyes fell upon it they opened wide in amazement. I also observed a trembling of his hand as he reached forth to touch it. He then recounted to me his marvellous adventure of the night before, but saying before he began:

"Thou knowest, O Prince, I am no believer in visions, and I should never tell the tale but for thy discovery of this cup. I drank from such an one last night, proffered by a ghostly hand."

I would have smiled, but he was much in earnest. As I made a movement to sit beside him, he said:

"Taste first, O my master, of the grapes hanging from yonder wall."

I did so, and to my great surprise found them of an exquisite flavor, finer even than the cultivated fruit of Persia, sweeter and more delicate, of a different nature from the wild grapes we have been eating. My astonishment appeared to delight him, and he said with a laugh:

"The grapes are impossible, but they exist; even more absurd is my story!" and he then narrated his adventure.

It was this:

WHAT LEV-EL-HEDYD SAW.

Yesterday, after nightfall, as he was hastening toward the *Zlōtuhb* he fell violently upon some blocks of stone, wrenching his ankle and much bruising himself. Unable to walk upon his foot he limped into this building to await our coming in the morning. The howling of wolves and other wild beasts as they prowled about the city drove him, for safety, to crawl up the ruins of the stairway to the floor above. As he settled himself in a corner of this hall his nostrils were greeted with the delicious odor from the grapes about his head. He found them surprisingly good, and ate heartily. He soon after fell into a sleep which lasted some hours, for when he awoke the moon was higher in the heavens, the voices of the wolves were hushed and the city was silent.

As he lay in a revery, much absorbed in his own thoughts, he gradually became aware of mysterious changes taking place, as if by stealth, about him. A decorated ceiling appeared to be closing over the hall. Mirrors and tinted walls slowly crept in place of ivy and crumbling bricks. A faint glow grew stronger and more intense until it filled the great room with a dazzling light.

Then came softly into view a table of curious form, set out with flowers and innu-

merable dishes of glass and porcelain, as for
a feast.

Standing about the room he saw solemn
men with beardless faces, all in black attire,
whose garments bore triangular openings upon
the chest to show the shirt beneath. These per-
sonages he soon discovered were servants.

As he gazed in bewilderment, there entered other figures, two by two, who took their
seats about the table. These later comers, sixty
or more, were men and women walking arm
in arm, the women in rich attire of unfamiliar
fashion and sparkling with precious stones.
The men were clad like the servants.

They ate and drank and laughed, and
formed a brilliant scene. Lev-el-Hedyd rose
to his feet, and moved by a curiosity he made
no effort to resist, — for he is a reckless fel-
low and knows no fear — he hobbled out into
the room.

They looked upon him in surprise, and
seemed much amused at his presence. One of
the guests, a tall youth with yellow mustach-

51

es, approached him, offering a delicate crystal vessel filled with a sparkling fluid.

Lev-el-Hedyd took it. The youth raised another from the table and with a slight gesture as if in salutation, he said in words which my comrade understood, though he swears it was a language unknown to him,

"We may meet again the fourth of next month."

He then drank the wine, and so did Lev-el-Hedyd.

Hereupon the others smiled as if at their comrade's wit, all save the women, whose tender faces spoke more of pity than of mirth. The wine flew to his brain as he drank it, and things about him seemed to reel and spin. Strains of fantastic music burst upon his ears: then, all in rhythm, the women joined their partners and whirled about him with a lightsome step. And, moving with it, his throbbing brain seemed dancing from his head. The room itself, all swaying and quivering with the melody, grew dim and stole from view. The music softly died away.

KUZUNDAM'S NARROW ESCAPE

Again was silence, the moon above looking calmly down upon the ivied walls.

He fell like a drunken man upon the floor, and did not wake till our voices called him.

Such his tale.

He has a clear head and is no liar, but so many grapes upon an empty stomach with the fever from his swollen limb might well explain it.

. . . .

Bear's meat for dinner.

This morning toward noon Kuzundam, the second officer, wandered on ahead of us, and entered a large building in pursuit of a rabbit. He was about descending to the basement below, when he saw, close before him, a bear leisurely mounting the marble stairs. Kuzundam is no coward, but he turned and ran as he never ran before. The bear, who seemed of a sportive nature, also ran, and in close pursuit. Luckily for my friend we happened to be near, otherwise instead of our eating bear's meat, the bear might have lunched quietly off Kuzundam in the shady corridors of the "FIFTHAVENUEHOTEL."

O-DAY a scorching heat that burns the lungs. We started in the morning prepared to spend the night ashore, and explore the northern end of the city. It was a pleas-ant walk through the soft grass of the shady streets, but in those places unsheltered from the sun we were as fish upon a frying-pan. Other dwellings we saw, even larger and more imposing than the one we entered yesterday. We were tempted to explore them, but Lev-el-Hedyd wisely dissuaded us, saying the day was waxing hotter each hour and it could be done on our return.

In the northern part of the town are many religious temples, with their tall towers like slender pyramids, tapering to a point. They are curious things, and surprisingly well preserved. The interiors of these temples are uninteresting. Nōfūhl says the religious rites of the Mehrikans were devoid of character. There were many religious beliefs, all complicated and insignificant variations one from another, each sect having its own temples and refusing to believe as the others. This is amusing to a Persian, but mayhap was a serious matter with them. One day in each week they assembled, the priests reading long moral lectures written by themselves, with music by hired singers. They then separated, taking no thought of temple or priest for another seven days. Nōfūhl says they were not a religious people. That the temples were filled mostly with women.

In the afternoon we found it necessary to traverse a vast pleasure-ground, now a wild forest, but with traces still visible of broad promenades and winding drive-ways.[1] There remains an avenue of bronze statues, most of

[1] Olbaldeh thinks this must be the Centralpahk sometimes alluded to in Mehrikan literature.

IN ONE OF THE TEMPLES

them yet upright and in good condition, but very comic. Lev-el-Hedyd and I still think them caricatures, but Nōfūhl is positive they were serious efforts, and says the Mehrikans were easily pleased in matters of art.

We lost our way in this park, having nothing to guide us as in the streets of the city. This was most happy, as otherwise we should have missed a surprising discovery.

It occurred in this wise.

Being somewhat overcome by the heat we halted upon a little hill to rest ourselves. While reclining beneath the trees I noticed unusual carvings upon a huge block against which Lev-el-Hedyd was supporting his back. They were unlike any we had seen, and yet they were not unfamiliar. As I lay there gazing idly at them it flashed upon me they were Egyptian. We at once fell to examining the block, and found to our amazement an obelisk of Egyptian granite, covered with Egyptian hieroglyphics of an antiquity exceeding by thousands of years the most ancient monuments of the country!

**"Miles away in the river lay the *Zlōtuhb*,
a white speck on the water."**

Verily, we were puzzled !

"When did the Egyptians invade Mehri-ka?" quoth Bhoz-jā-khāz, with a solemn look, as if trying to recall a date.

"No Egyptian ever heard of Mehrika," said Nōfūhl. "This obelisk was finished twenty centuries before the first Mehrikan was weaned. In all probability it was brought here as a curiosity, just as we take to Persia the bronze head of George-wash-yn-tun."

We spent much time over the monument, and I think Nōfūhl was disappointed that he could not bring it away with him.

Also while in this park we came to a high tower, standing by itself, and climbed to the top, where we enjoyed a widespreading view.

The extent of the city is astounding.

Miles away in the river lay the *Zlōtuhb*, a white speck on the water. All about us in every direction as far as sight can reach were ruins, and ruins, and ruins. Never was a more melancholy sight. The blue sky, the bright sunshine, the sweet-scented air with the gay flowers and singing birds only made it sadder. They seemed a mockery.

We have encamped for the night, and I can write no more. Countless flying insects gather about us with a hateful buzz, and bite us beyond endurance. They are a pest thrice accursed.

I tell Nōfūhl his fine theory concerning the extinction of the Yahnkis is a good tale for those who have never been here.

No man without a leather skin could survive a second night.

18th May

POOR Jā-khāz is worse than sick.

He had an encounter last night with a strange animal, and his defeat was ignoble. The animal, a pretty thing, much like a kitten, was hovering near when Jā-khāz, with rare courage and agility, threw himself upon it.

And then what happened none of us can state with precision. We know we held our noses and fled. And Jā-khāz! No words can fit him. He carries with him an odor to devastate a province. We had to leave him ashore and send him fresh raiment.

This is, verily, a land of surprises.

Our hands and faces still smart from the

biting insects, and the perfume of the odorous kitten promises to be ever with us.

Nōfūhl is happy. We have discovered hundreds of metal blocks, the poorest of which he asserts would be the gem of a museum. They were found by Fattan-laïz-eh in the basement of a high building, all laid carefully away upon iron shelves. The flood of light they throw upon the manners and customs of this ludicrous people renders them of priceless value to historians.

I harbor a suspicion that it causes Nōfūhl some pleasure to sit upon the cool deck of the *Zlōtuhb* and watch Bhoz-jā-khāz walking to and fro upon the ruins of a distant wharf.

THE LAST AMERICAN

19ᵗʰ MAY

19th May

HE air is cooler. Grip-til-lah thinks a storm is brewing.

Even Nōfūhl is puzzled over the wooden image we brought aboard yesterday. It is well preserved, with the barbaric coloring still fresh upon it. They found it standing upright in a little shop.

How these idols were worshipped, and why they are found in little shops and never in the great temples is a mystery. It has a diadem of feathers on the head, and as we sat smoking upon the deck this evening I remarked to Nōfūhl that it might be the portrait of some Mehrikan noble. Whereupon he said they had no nobles.

"But the Mehrikans of gentle blood," I asked, "had they no titles?"

"Neither titles nor gentle blood," he answered. "And as they were all of much the same origin, and came to this country simply

THE WOODEN GOD.

to thrive more fatly than at home, there was nothing except difference in wealth on which to establish a superior order. Being deep respecters of money this was a satisfying distinction. It soon resulted that those families

A Street Scene in Ancient Nhū-Yok

(The costumes and manner of riding are taken from metal plates now in the museum at Teheran.)

who possessed riches for a generation or two became the substitute for an aristocracy. This upper class was given to sports and pastimes, spending their wealth freely, being prodigiously fond of display. Their intellectual development was feeble, and they wielded but little influence save in social matters. They followed closely the fashions of foreign aristocracies. Great attentions were paid to wandering nobles from other lands. Even distant relatives of titled people were greeted with the warmest enthusiasm."

Then I said to him, "But explain to me, O Nōfūhl, how it was possible for so shallow a nation to become so great."

"They were great only in numbers and too weak to endure success. At the beginning of the twentieth century — as they counted time — huge fortunes were amassed in a day, and the Mehrikans became drunk with money."

Whereupon I exclaimed, "O Land of Delight! For much money is cheering."

But the old man shook his head. "Very

true, O Prince; but the effect was woeful. These vast fortunes soon dominated all things, even the seat of government and the courts of Justice. Tricks of finance brought fabulous gains. Young men became demoralized. For sober industry with its moderate profits was ridiculed."

"Verily, that would be natural!" I said. "But in a land where all were rich who was found to cook and scrub, to fetch and carry and to till the soil? For none will shovel earth when his pockets are stuffed with gold."

"All were not rich. And when the poor also became greedy they became hostile. Then began social upheavals with bloodshed and havoc."

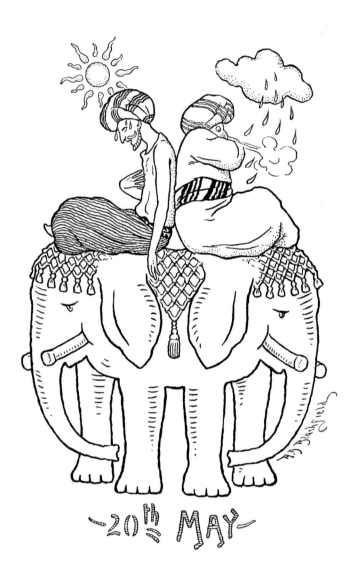

20th May

N icy wind from the north-east with a violent rain. Yesterday we gasped with the hot air. To-day we are shivering in winter clothing.

21st May

HE same as yesterday. Most of us are ill. My teeth chatter and my body is both hot and cold. A storm more wicked never wailed about a ship. Lev-el-Hedyd calls it the shrieking voices of the hundred millions of Mehrikans who must have perished in similar weather.

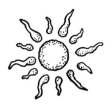

16th June

T is many days since I have touched this journal. A hateful sickness has been upon me, destroying all energy and courage. A sort of fever, and yet my limbs were cold. I could not describe it if I would.

Nōfūhl came into the cabin this evening with some of his metal plates and discoursed upon them. He has no respect for the intellects of the early Mehrikans. I thought for a moment I had caught him in a contradiction, but he was right as usual. It was thus:

Nōfūhl.

They were great readers.

Khan-li.

You have told us they had no literature. Were they great readers of nothing?

Nōfūhl.

Verily, thou hast said it! Vast sheets of paper were published daily in which all crimes were recorded in detail. The more revolting the deed, the more minute the description. Horrors were their chief delight. Scandals were drunk in with thirstful eyes. These chronicles of crime and filth were issued by hundreds of thousands. There was hardly a family in the land but had one.

Khan-li.

And did this take the place of literature?

Nōfūhl.

Even so.

The Last American

20th June

NCE more we are on the sea; two days from Nhū-Yok. Our decision was a sudden one. Nōfūhl, in an evil moment, found among those accursed plates a map of the country, and thereupon was seized with an unreasoning desire to visit a town called "Washington." I wavered and at last consented, foolishly I believe, for the crew are loud for Persia. And this town is inland on a river. He says it was their finest city, the seat of Government, the capital of the country. Grip-til-lah swears he can find it if the map is truthful.

Jā-khāz still eats by himself.

This afternoon we reclined upon the deck, the *Zlōtuhb* drifting gently in a southerly direction. Land could be seen on the starboard bow, a faint strip along the western horizon.

It was about the middle of the afternoon, while passing the ruins of a gigantic tower — perhaps a lighthouse — that Nōfŭhl, of a sudden, clambered hastily to his feet and looked about him. Then he called to Grip-til-lah, asking how many leagues we were from the harbor of Nhū-Yok. Grip-til-lah's reply I forget, but it filled the old man with a gentle excitement. I observed an unwonted sparkle in his eyes, also a quivering of the fingers as he pointed to the ocean around about, and exclaimed —

"Beneath us, the bottom of the sea is covered with iron ships — the wrecks of stupendous navies — the mightiest of all human history!"

At once we all became interested.

"What navies?" I inquired. "And what compassed their destruction? Was it a battle?"

Nōfūhl.

A battle of whose magnitude no Persian has conception; a conflict in which the sea was tossed and the heavens rent by thunderings of iron monsters. Any one of them would have blown to atoms a fleet of *Zlōtuhbs*.

Ad-el-pate.

Verily! A tale easier told than believed. But I would readily venture my head in the *Zlōtuhb* against any of these nursery-tale wonders.

Nōfūhl.

And with wisdom. For the loss of thy brain, Ad-el-pate, could not affect the nature of thy speech. Whereupon there was laughter, and Ad-el-pate held his peace.

Khan-li.

But tell us of this battle, O Nōfūhl. I remember now to have read about it at college. These details of ancient history I am prone to forget. How came it about?

Nōfūhl.

I have spoken of the Mehrikans being a greedy race. And their greed, at last, resulted in this war. By means of one-sided laws of their own making they secured for themselves a lion's share of all profits from the world's commerce. This checked the prosperity of other nations, until at last the leading powers of Europe combined in self-defence against this all-absorbing greed. They collected an armada the like of which was never imagined, neither before nor since. Then, across the ocean, came the iron host. And here, upon this very spot where we are floating, they met the Mehrikan ships.

Khan-li.

How many ships in all?

Nōfūhl.

The Mehrikans had eighty heavy ships of iron, with a number of smaller craft. The allies had two hundred and forty heavy battle-ships, all of iron. They also had smaller craft for diverse purposes.

Khan-li.

Allah! A bad prospect for our greedy friends! And being a nation of traders they had no liking, probably, for the perils of war.

Nōfūhl.

As to that historians differ. According to the Mehrikans themselves they were mighty warriors. But certain writers of that period give a different impression. Nōz-yt-ahl is sure they were cowards, weak in body as in spirit, but often favored by fortune. In my opinion, this battle throws considerable light upon that matter. A day like this, it was, also in June, as the Europeans, coming northward along the coast to seize Nhū-Yok, met the Mehrikan Admiral Nev-r-sai-di with his eighty ships. And the struggle was short.

Khan-li.

Verily, I can believe it! With three ships to one I would give the Europeans about half a day — a summer afternoon like this — to send the greedy ones to the bottom.

Nōfūhl.

Thy guess is good, O Prince, as to the hours of fighting. It lasted just one summer afternoon. But the Mehrikans it was who sent their enemies to the bottom. And the sea beneath our feet is strewn with iron hulks.

Khan-ti.

Bismillah! If that be a true tale — and I doubt it not — these greedy ones were not so contemptible, at least when there was profit in it.

Lev-el-Hedyd.

At what period did this occur?

Nōfūhl.

Early in the twentieth century. I cannot recall the date, but it was never forgotten by the Mehrikans. Surely a just pride, for on that day they accomplished wonders. The Admiral Nev-r-sai-di on his ship the *Ztazenztrypes* was at one time surrounded by a dozen German men-of-war. And lo! he demolished all! And of Frank and Russyan vessels he put an end to as many more; also sundry Talyans and British.

Lev-el-Hedyd.

Bismillah! But that was good! What, O Nōfūhl, is the Persian of that name *Ztazenz-trypes*?

Nōfūhl.

None can tell with certainty. To the Mehrikans it signified victory, or something similar.

Other miracles were achieved by the Mehrikans that day. *Nōfli-zon-mee*, a little craft with a pointed prow, jammed holes in nearly a score of monster ships, and the waters closed over them. There figured also a long and narrow boat of Mehrikan devising, the *Yankyd-Oodl*. This astonishing machine sailed to and fro among the foreign ships upsetting all traditions. Much glory befell her commander, the Captain Hoorai-boiz.

Grip-til-lah.

And how many ships did the Mehrikans lose?

Nōfūhl.

Reports are contradictory. According to one of their own writers of the period they suffered no loss whatever in vessels. Yet at the same time he asserts, "We gave them Haleklumbya," which must be the name of a ship.

Khan-li.

A gallant fight! But can you explain how such an interior people could become heroic of a sudden?

Nōfūhl.

According to 'Ardfax, an early British historian, they were addicted to surprising feats upon the water. And this statement is borne out by a Spanish admiral, Offulbad-shoota, who maintains that the Mehrikans, being a godless people, were aided by the devil.

THE LAST AMERICAN

 E are on the river that leads to "Washington." Grip-til-lah says we shall sight it to-morrow. The river is a dirty color.

3d July

E see ahead of us the ruins of a great dome, also a very high shaft. Probably they belong to the city we seek.

THE LAST AMERICAN

"We see ahead of us the ruins of a great dome,
also a very high shaft."

DATE we shall not forget!

Little did I realize this morning when we left the *Zlōtuhb* in such hilarious mood what dire events awaited us. I landed about noon, accompanied by Nōfūhl, Lev-el-Hedyd, Bhoz-jā-khāz, Ad-el-pate, Kuzundam the first mate, Tik'l-palyt the cook, Fattan-laïz-eh, and two sailors. Our march had scarce begun when a startling discovery caused great commotion in our minds. We had halted at Nōfūhl's request, to decipher the inscription upon a stone, when Lev-el-Hedyd, who had started on, stopped short with a sudden exclamation. We hastened to him, and there, in the soft earth, was the imprint of human feet!

I cannot describe our surprise. We decided to follow the footprints, and soon found they were leading us toward the great dome more directly than we could have gone ourselves.

Through the Streets of "Washington."

Our excitement was beyond words. Those of us who had weapons carried them in readiness. The path was little used, but clearly marked. It wound about among fallen fragments and crumbling statues, and took us along a wide avenue between buildings of vast size and so-

"He remained in the same position, not even withdrawing his feet."

lidity, far superior to any we had seen in Nhū-Yok. It seemed a city of monuments.

As we ascended the hill to the great temple and saw it through the trees rising high above us, we were much impressed by its vast size and beauty. Our eyes wandered in admiration over the massive columns, each hewn from a single block, still white and fresh as if newly quarried. The path took us under one of the lower arches of the building, and we emerged upon the other side. This front we found even more beautiful than the one facing the city. At the centre was a flight of steps of magnificent proportions, now falling asunder and overgrown in many places with grass and flowers.

These steps we ascended. As I climbed silently up, the others following, I saw two human feet, the soles toward us, resting upon the balustrade above. With a gesture I directed Nōfūhl's attention to them, and the old man's eyes twinkled with delight. Was it a Mehrikan? I confess to a lively excitement at the prospect of meeting one. How many were

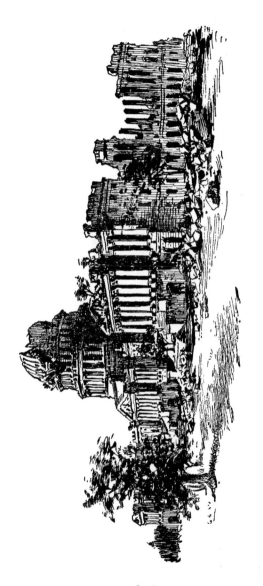

THE RUINS OF THE GREAT TEMPLE

they? and how would they treat us?

Looking down upon my little band to see that all were there, I boldly marched up the remaining steps and stood before him.

THE FEET UPON THE PORTICO.

He was reclining upon a curious little four-legged seat, with his feet upon the balustrade, about on a level with his head. Clad in skins

104

and rough cloth he looked much like a hunter, and he gazed quietly upon me, as though a Persian noble were a daily guest. Such a reception was not gratifying, especially as he remained in the same position, not even withdrawing his feet. He nodded his curious head down once and up again, deeming it apparently a sufficient salutation.

The maintenance of my own dignity before my followers forbade my standing thus before a seated barbarian, and I made a gesture for him to rise. This he answered in an unseemly manner by ejecting from his mouth a brownish fluid, projecting it over and beyond the balustrade in front of him. Then looking upon me as if about to laugh, and yet with a grave face, he uttered something in an unmusical voice which I failed to understand.

Upon this Nōfūhl, who had caught the meaning of one or two words, stepped hastily forward and addressed him in his own language. But the barbarian understood with difficulty and they had much trouble in conversing, chiefly from reason of Nōfūhl's pronunciation. He afterward told me that this man's language differed but little from that of the Mehrikans, as they wrote it eleven centuries ago.

When he finally arose in talking with Nōfūhl I could better observe him. He was tall and bony, with an awkward neck, and appeared at first glance to be a man of forty years. We decided later he was under thirty. His yellow skin and want of hair made him seem much older than he was. I was also much puzzled by the expression of his face. It was one of deep sadness, yet his eyes were full of mirth, and a corner of his mouth was ever drawing up as if in mockery. For myself I liked not his manner. He appeared little impressed by so many strangers, and bore himself as though it were of small importance whether we understood him or not. But Nōfūhl since informed me that he asked a multitude of questions concerning us.

What Nōfūhl gathered was this:

This Mehrikan with his wife and one old man were all that remained of his race. Thirty-one had died this summer. In ancient times there were many millions of his country-men. They were the greatest nation upon the earth.

THE MAN

He could not read. He had two names, one was "Jon," the other he had forgotten. They lived in this temple because it was cool. When the temple was built, and for what purpose, he could not tell. He pointed to the West and said the country in that direction was covered with ruined cities.

When Nōfūhl told him we were friends, and presented him at my direction with a hunting-knife of fine workmanship, he pushed out his right arm toward me and held it there. For an instant Nōfūhl looked at the arm wonderingly, as did we all, then with sudden intelligence he seized the outstretched hand in his own, and moved it up and down. This was interesting, for Nōfūhl tells me it was a form of greeting among the ancient Mehrikans.

While all this was going on we had moved into the great circular hall beneath the dome. This hall was of vast proportions, and there were still traces of its former splendor. Against the walls were marble statues entwined in ivy, looking down upon us with melancholy eyes. Here also we met a thin old man, whose hairless head and beardless face almost moved us to mirth.

At Nōfūhl's request our host led the way into some of the smaller rooms to show us their manner of living, and it would be impossible to imagine a more pathetic mixture of glory and decay, of wealth and poverty, of civilization and barbarity. Old furniture, dishes of silver, bronze images, even paintings and ornaments of great value were scattered through the rooms, side by side with the most primitive implements. It was plain the ancient arts were long since forgotten.

When we returned to the circular hall our host disappeared for a few moments into a room which he had not shown us. He came back bringing a stone vase with a narrow neck, and was followed by a maiden who bore drinking-cups of copper and tin. These she deposited upon a fallen fragment of the dome which served as a table.

This girl was interesting. A dainty head, delicate features, yellow hair, blue eyes, and a gentle sadness of mien that touched my heart. Had she been ugly what a different ending to this day!

We all saluted her, and the Mehrikan

spoke a few words which we interpreted as a presentation. He filled the cups from the stone vase, and then saying something which Nōfūhl failed to catch, he held his cup before his face with a peculiar movement and put it to his lips. As he did this Lev-el-Hedyd clutched my arm and exclaimed:

"The very gesture of the ghost!"

And then as if to himself, "And this is July fourth."

But he drank, as did we all, for our thirst was great and the odor of the golden liquid was most alluring. It tasted hotter than the fires of Jelbuz. It was also of great potency and gave a fine exhilaration to the senses. We became happier at once.

And here it was that Jā-khāz did a fatal thing. Being near the maid and much affected by her beauty, he addressed her as *Hur-al-missa*,[1] which, of course, she understood not. This were well had he gone no further, but he next put his arm about her waist with intent to kiss her. Much terrified, she tried to free her-

[1] The most angelic of women.

110

self. But Jā-khāz, holding her fair chin with his other hand, had brought his lips almost to hers when the old man raised his heavy staff and brought it down upon our comrade's head with cruel swiftness. This falling stick upon a solid skull resounded about the dome and echoed through the empty corridors.

Bhoz-jā-khāz blinked and staggered back.

Then, with fury in his face, he sprang savagely toward the aged man.

But here the younger Mehrikan interfered. Rapidly approaching them and shutting tight his bony hand, he shot it from him with startling velocity, so directing that it came in contact with the face of Jā-khāz who, to our amazement, sat roughly upon the marble pavement, the blood streaming from his nostrils. He was a pitiful sight.

Unaccustomed to such warfare we were seriously alarmed, and thought him killed perhaps. Ad-el-pate, a mighty wrestler, and of powerful build, rushed furiously upon the Mehrikan for whom I trembled. But his arm again went out before him, and Ad-el-pate likewise sat. A mournful spectacle, and every Persian felt his heart beat fast within him.

By this time Jā-khāz was on his feet again, purple with rage. With uplifted scimitar he sprang toward our host. The old man stepped between. Jā-khāz, with wanton cruelty, brought his steel upon the ancient head, and stretched him upon the floor. For an instant the younger one stood horror-stricken, then snatching from the floor the patriarch's staff — a heavy stick with an iron end — he jumped forward, and, quicker than words can tell it, dealt a frightful blow upon the head of Jā-khāz which sent him headlong to the ground with a broken skull.

All this had happened in a moment, and wild confusion followed. My followers drew their arms and rushed upon the Mehrikan. The girl ran forward either from terror or to shield her spouse, I know not which, when a flying arrow from a sailor's cross-bow pierced her to the heart.

This gave the Mehrikan the energy of twenty men.

THE SLAUGHTER OF THE PERSIANS

He knocked brave Kuzundam senseless with a blow that would have killed an ox. Such fury I had not conceived. He brought his flying staff like a thunderbolt from Heaven upon the Persian skulls, yet always edging toward the door to prevent his enemies surrounding him. Four of our number, in as many minutes, joined Jā-khāz upon the floor. Kuzundam, Ad el-pate, Fattan-laïz-eh, and Hä-tak, a sailor, lay stretched upon the pavement, all dead or grievously wounded.

So suddenly had this taken place, that I hardly realized what had happened. I rushed forward to stay the combat, but he mistook the purpose, struck my scimitar with a force that sent it flying through the air, and had raised his staff to deal a second for myself, when brave Lev-el-Hedyd stepped in to save me, and thrust quickly at him. But alas! the Mehrikan warded off his stroke with one yet quicker, and brought his stick so swiftly against my comrade's head that it laid him with the others.

When Lev-el-Hedyd fell I saw the Mehrikan had many wounds, for my comrades had made a savage onslaught. He tottered as he

THE LAST OF THE MEHRIKANS

moved back into the doorway, where he leaned against the wall for an instant, his eyes meeting ours with a look of defiance and contempt that I would willingly forget. Then the staff dropped from his hand; he staggered out to the great portico, and fell his length upon the pavement. Nōfūhl hastened to him, but he was dead.

As he fell a wonderful thing took place — an impossible thing, as I look back upon it, but both Nōfūhl and I saw it distinctly.

In front of the great steps and facing this doorway is a large sitting image of George-wash-yn-tun. As the Mehrikan staggered out upon the porch, his hands outstretched before him and with Death at his heart, this statue slowly bowed its head as if in recognition of a gallant fight.

Perhaps it was the sorrowful acceptance of a bitter ending.

"This statue slowly bowed its head."

11th July

GAIN upon the sea.

This time for Persia, bearing our wounded and the ashes of the dead; those of the natives are reposing beneath the Great Temple.

The skull of the last Mehrikan I shall present to the museum at Teheran.